LOVE BEYOND LIFETIME

SANDIP CHATTERJEE

Copyright © Sandip Chatterjee
All Rights Reserved.

This book has been published with all efforts taken to make the material error-free after the consent of the author. However, the author and the publisher do not assume and hereby disclaim any liability to any party for any loss, damage, or disruption caused by errors or omissions, whether such errors or omissions result from negligence, accident, or any other cause.

While every effort has been made to avoid any mistake or omission, this publication is being sold on the condition and understanding that neither the author nor the publishers or printers would be liable in any manner to any person by reason of any mistake or omission in this publication or for any action taken or omitted to be taken or advice rendered or accepted on the basis of this work. For any defect in printing or binding the publishers will be liable only to replace the defective copy by another copy of this work then available.

This one is dedicated to "Love of My Life".

Contents

Foreword

First published book is very special. I want to thank each one who believed in me.

Preface

Sandip is born and brought up in a small village near Kolkata. From his childhood, stories fascinate him. He always believed in the transcendence of written words.

Prologue

1. **Final Call**

A love story beyond religious barriers. Will Love sail through or it will drown the lovers with it.

2. The Shoot of Fate

Inspired by a true incident. How an unforeseen situation changes the course of a person's life.

3. **Last Day**

A sci fi Love story framed on the future time line when we will be able to know our loved one's last days.

4. **The Unsung Heroes**

In the dilemma between love and responsibility, what did our unsung heroes choose. A special tribute to the covid warriors and their sacrifices.

5. **The Incomplete Painting**

A modern-day love story in the ghats of Kashi. Will the incomplete painting be able to complete two people.

I

Final Call

It was 2 AM in the night when Usha tiptoed out of the front door. She reached the end of the lane and turned to take one last look at the house that she lived in for the last 24 years, since her birth. The bag in her hand felt heavy, just like her feet. She dropped the bag on the side of the road and opened the front zip of her handbag which was hanging from her right shoulder. She took out the phone and dialed Arif's number. She remembered it by heart.

The phone rang its full ring tone but, no one responded.

She called once again and waited for the ring to finish. Still no response.

"I m gng to the bus stop alone. Come fast pls" - She typed the message, sent in what's app and kept the phone back into her handbag in a hurry.

She dragged the trolly bag by her left hand and started walking down the dark road.

It was a typical winter night, a windy one, where you struggle to breathe because of the cold wind thrashing on her face. Moreover, she was underprepared for the cold. She kept walking through the dark road pulling her shawl tighter, hiding her face. The lonely roads on a winter night felt, even more, lonelier to her. There were a few dogs on the side of the road, but even they didn't bother to shout at her.

The street lights were uneven. Some places were having lights though it was not clearly visible due to the fog, and some parts were pitch dark.

She kept walking, hoping that the dog would not bark or run behind her. She has walked many times in this road before. She remembered how she always used to hide behind her father whenever dogs used to come close. In the darkness of the night, all her memories were clear and bright. She remembered how her father taught her how to ride a bicycle. Every Monday, how she used to walk in this lane with her mom to go to the nearby temple. It felt like yesterday.

But tonight, was completely different. she was alone. She chose to set forth in her own journey.

With a few steps, she would stop to breathe and look back to see her home. Her house was still visible until she reached the end of the straight road, from where she had to take a left turn to go towards the bus stop. She stopped for a while, turned back, and saw her house one last time. She could see the blue night lamp on the balcony. She did not know if what she was doing is right or wrong, but at this moment, this was the only thing she could do for herself, for her love. She didn't even know when she would be coming back to her home again. Even, she was not sure if she would be able to come back at all or not.

She knew society will never accept it but she was more concerned about her parents. Will they accept this love marriage? Will they agree?

All these thoughts were running through her mind. Her tears started rolling down her cheek. She held herself tightly and tightened her jacket and affirmed herself –

'This is not the time to look back. You have to be strong and move ahead, for your love. For Arif'

She turned back and started walking towards the bus stop holding the phone in her hand. She dialed Arif's number once again and it was switched off.

Arif

The last time Arif talked to Usha was in the evening, she was crying while telling him how her parents are forcing her to marry Prakash. She explained how she tried to tell them about him at home, but they were furious listening to his name. Arif was calm and was listening to everything very carefully. He consoled her and asked her not to worry, they will find something to work it out, as always. But he also knew very well that this situation is not like any other. She was not listening to anything, continuously crying.

"Usha, listen, listen, don't cry, please. Stop. Please" – Arif begged her.

"I can't live with anyone else for the rest of my life. I will die of guilt and regret. It's better I die now" – she busted out in tears.

"Shuu!! Stop it. Don't talk rubbish" – he scolded her.

"tell me please, what to do. I can't live without you" – she requested him.

He was silent. He knew there were not many options left on their hands now.

"I will come out of my home. Let's see how can they stop us" – there was rage in her voice, but more than that, there was resolution.

"But" – Arif tried to suggest something but was interrupted by Usha in the middle.

"I will be waiting for you Arif. Don't prove me wrong. Please" – she told very firmly and cut the call.

Arif's Home

Arif came back from college, a little late that day. His final date of submission of the Ph.D. paper was coming near. Arif's elder sister, Atifa, was home that evening. Atifa was very close to Arif. Arif decided to talk to Atifa about Usha. He believed that she would definitely understand him and more importantly support him. He needed her to support the most at that time. Atif trusted her and told everything to her, including the plan of eloping together. Atifa was in shock and became silent. She looked at her younger brother and did not even say a word. Atifa came out of the room silently and did not even turn back. While Arif waited alone in that dark room.

The situation at home was awkwardly silent. The uneasy look of his parents over the dinner table was suggesting that the news had reached them through Atifa. Arif was waiting for someone else to bring up the topic. But everyone kept quiet.

He finished his dinner in a hurry and went straight to his room. He did not want to face anyone. He was waiting for Usha's call eagerly sitting on his bed.

After some time, Atifa pushed the door and came inside.

"Give me your phone, I need to make a call" - she asked firmly.

"Abbu told anything?" - he asked in anticipation while taking out the phone from his pocket.

There was a blank expression on her face, she did not say anything. She just took the phone and came out of his room. While coming out, she locked the room from the outside. Arif was locked in his own room.

On The Bus Stop

Ush was waiting for Arif at the bus stop, holding her phone and calling his number continuously.

It was the same response from the other side of the phone - 'The number you are calling is currently switched off. Kindly try after some time.

With every passing moment, the anxiety inside her was rising. Every headlight of the bikes from the main road was filling her with anticipation of Arif. She waited at the bus stop for 15 minutes and kept dialing Arif's switched-off number.

After few more failed attempts, when she was almost on the verge of giving up. She saw a bike coming towards her. She stood up from her place. Even in the dim street light, she recognized the bike immediately. It was Arif's father's bike, the one Arif used. She was relieved. She waved her hand towards the bike. The bike took a turn and came towards her when she realized, it's not Arif.

The bike stopped right in front of her. She tried to ignore the person.

"Arif bhajan sent me to pick you up from the bus stand. His phone is switched off. He is waiting in a car near the flyover." - the middle-aged guy who was driving the bike told Usha without removing his helmet, while showing Arif's contact on his phone. Usha could see Arif's face in his phone, the glowing smile wearing the shirt she gifted on his last birthday. The guy looked to be in a hurry and wanted her to come with him. Usha did not have any other choice. She wanted to call Arif once. She wanted to reach to Arif by any means. She kept the bag between and sat on the bike. The guy took a sharp turn and drove through the dark road.

News Headline Next Day: -

Allahabad is on the verge of communal rights. A Hindu girl was beheaded and her lifeless body was thrown beside the road. Police assumed an inter-religion love affair as the reason for the killing. The entire Hindu community is raging over the brutal murder of their daughter. One person named; Arif Mohammad was taken into custody. Police are on red alert amidst the high tension.

II

The Shoot of Fate

The flight home was already delayed by 3 hours and the exact announcement of its departure was yet to come. The queue of impatient passengers was wandering in front of the announcement gate. Eagerly waiting for the latest announcement of their flights.

The radiant advertisement screen was showing -

"Welcome to Tehran International Airport. You are safe here".

"I am not a refugee; I am an immigrant" – A almost thirty years of old tall and the suited guy said with a tone of irritation rather than explanation. The immigration officer did not seem to be convinced though.

"Please wait outside, Mr. Ali" – told the officer, while picking up his phone to call his higher officials.

Ali heaved a sigh and came out of the room pushing the glass door. His phone was still vibrating in the right pocket of his blue denim.

He was exhausted with the entire immigration process. He walked towards the entrance gate holding his trolly in one hand and file of papers in the other. He sat on an empty chair in one corner of the airport lawn. He could see the airplanes standing in a queue waiting for their turn to fly.

The phone started vibrating again, he picked up the call in a hurry.

"Hello, Abbu!!, I was at the immigration center" - he replied in a hurry sensing the tension on the other side of the phone.

"Is everything alright there?" – the question came with an obvious answer of no. But he was silent.

Ali hid all his worries and told almost calmly, "Yes, the flight should depart in some time."

"We saw the news of the assassination of Kasem Sulemani. We all are worried about the situation." – his worried father told.

"Yes, things are a little complicated here. Don't worry Abbu, I will be there in a few hours" – Ali assured his father.

"How is Ammi's health now" – he tried to divert the topic, which seemed to be the right thing to do at that moment.

His father passed the phone to his mom.

"Ammi, how is your health? Did you take the medicine before food?" – Ali asked enquiringly.

"How are you beta, why is your flight delayed? We are all worried here, please come back safe" – a frightened mother pleaded.

"I will be there sometime, please take care of yourself Mom" – Ali faked a forced smile, the first time, in the last few hours.

The voice of his mom reduced his tension a little bit.

'The boarding for Boeing 752 will start in 10 mins

– the announcement came finally with a sigh of relief for all the passengers waiting eagerly to get out of this Hell.

Followed by another announcement: -

"Mr. Ali Bakar, please report to the immigration center immediately."

"Mom, boarding is getting started, I will be there in 4 hours. I will call you after getting down in Ukraine. Please don't worry." – Ali told with great relief in his voice and some sense of certainty.

"I Love You Mom".

Ali went to the immigration center in a hurry. He was expecting another round of investigation from the officer. But to his surprise, the receptionist gave his visa with a smile,

"Have a safe journey" – the lady wished with a vibrant smile.

"Thank You" – Ali replied with a tired smile.

After getting out of the immigration office, he took out the phone and called Saba, while standing in the longboarding queue.

"Hey Hello, what's up" – Ali asked excitedly.

"Where are you, I was trying to reach out to you, how are you." – Saba almost broke into tears.

"Ahaa...You missed me?" – Ali teased.

"I don't miss anyone" – She lied.

"Ohh, I see. That's sad to know" – Ali replied with a flower-like smile in the middle of iron-breaking tension.

"The flight got delayed. Boarding started finally, I am in the queue," – he continued.

"Why this much late, is everything fine there" – She asked.

"Yes, everything is alright, I will be there in 4 hours. Then you don't have to miss me anymore." – Ali pinches her once again.

"Please take care of yourself, come back soon. I miss you" - Saba replied.

"I love you" – Ali kissed his engagement ring.

"I love you too".

"I will call you once I get down, Bye Now" – Ali told.

"Come Safe".

Ali smiled and kept the phone in his pocket.

The boarding queue became smaller now.

"It's time to go, finally"- he thought to himself while standing in the last of the queue.

He went inside the aircraft and searched for his window seat – 13A.

There was the silence of a graveyard inside the aircraft. Other passengers were searching for their seats quietly. There were worries, tension, and exhaustion on everyone's faces.

13B was still empty.

Ali kept his handbag on that seat and opened his phone. He saw a text message from Rubina.

'I am sorry that you had to go through all these just to attend my marriage. I can't believe you had to take this much to see me getting married to someone else. You deserve all of it though.'

Next message:

'But, really, Thank You so much for coming, it really means a lot to me. I have told you before also, but I feel like telling it now for one last time, I LOVE YOU. I may have to spend the rest of my life with someone else, but still, I will LOVE only YOU.'

There were a few more messages. Ali smiled and scrolled down.

"I will always be there in your life as a best friend, just like old times, before we both fell in love."

"Stay happy and keep smiling as always, it's the smiling face for which my heart had fallen. I will miss you so much.

See You soon in Ukraine".

'Cabin Crew please be seated for take-off; Boing 752 is ready to fly. Please keep your phone in Airplane mode. Apologies for the Delay' – The announcement of the pilot bought him back to reality.

Ali looked up from his phone to see a seven years old boy standing in front of him.

"Can you please exchange your seat with mine, I want to watch an airplane taking off the ground for the first time" – the little one requested with such intense innocence that can't be put down.

Ali smiled at the small package of happiness and replied, "Sure, I would love to do that".

"What's your name" – Ali asked while waking up from his window seat.

"Imtiaz Ansari" he hurriedly sat on the seat. He was already looking out from the small window.

Ali adjusted his things and sat on the beside seat. He opened his phone and read Rubina's messages one more time.

He typed -

'Anything for you. Don't worry, I am fine. I will call you once I reach home. It was great to see you getting married. Wish you a very happy married life. I love you too'.

Ali stopped before pressing the send button.

He thought for a moment and replaced "I Love You", with "I Miss You" and sent.

"Kindly switch off your cell phone Sir, the flight is taking off" – a young flight attendant requested Ali.

He nodded in acknowledgment. He opened Rubina's contact and typed "I Love You".

This time, he pressed send without a second thought. He switched off his phone and kept it in his pocket. He leaned towards Imtiaz and tightened his seat belt,

"Now you are ready to fly" – he smiled while Imtiaz was still gazing outside.

He fastened his own seatbelt and looked at the sky above the little one's head. There were a few dark clouds gathering up in the right corner of the sky. He was seeing those black clouds covering the empty parts of the sky, slowly. The butterfly on his stomach was indicating that he is on air now.

He was seeing the dark clouds coming nearer now. He closed his eyes peacefully for the first time in the entire day.

Ukraine International Airlines flight 752 crashes shortly after taking off from Tehran's airport, killing all 176 people aboard. Most passengers are Iranian and Iranian-Canadian, and the crew is Ukrainian. Iran was on high alert after Major General Qasem Soleimani's assassination. In a desperate urge to fight back, Iran mistakenly shot down the airplane. Iran's government apologizes for the mistake.

III

Last Day

I waited outside the airport gate, watching her enter the check-in counter with a suitcase in her one hand and passport in the other. The black jacket I gifted her on our third anniversary, was tied to her waist.

She turned back to check if I am still standing outside looking at her. It has always been our way of saying goodbye. When I used to go to drop her at her office, I used to wait for her to go inside and when she reached the main gate she used to turn back every time and wave at me. I used to wave back and then start towards my office. Even after being together for 5 years, still, this used to be our daily ritual. One time I was in a hurry and did not wait for her to enter the office, and as a result, she did not talk to me for two days.

Now that I was seeing her for the last time, I could not believe I let her go away from me. I wish I could have stopped her. I wish I could have hugged her for a few more minutes. I would listen and feel her warm breath on my neck for a little longer. I wish I could kiss her one last time. I would hold my arms around her waist and pull her closer to mine. One Last Time. I was already missing her so much.

I did not have any choice though. I can't afford to go with her. There should be someone to take care of our daughter.

"Mamma will be back in two days" – Rebecca kissed our nine-year-old daughter Emilie.

I was standing behind her and watching the little one hugging her mom tightly.

"And, Papa will be back in an hour. Then we will play video games and make a cake and we won't give it to mommy" – I told her while taking her in my lap. And I whispered at my wife - "Rebecca it's getting late for the flight".

The babysitter took Emilie in her lap and took her to play so that she forgets about us for some time.

"Let's go" – Rebecca took her luggage and closed the door softly. Her eyes were wet. I could imagine how hard it was for her to leave both of us for six months. But I knew how badly she wanted this role and how much she has worked on this project. And, I wanted to stand strong beside her and give her wings the strength so that she can fly.

We sat in the car and started towards the airport. One of our friends was driving, I was sitting in the front seat and she was sitting in the back seat with her luggage. I was reminding her about a few important last-minute things and she was making sure everything was there in the luggage.

We were halfway down the road when I got a notification on my phone. It was an unusual alert. I ignored it at first as Rebecca was giving me a few tips about how to feed Emilie. It again started ringing in a minute. It interrupted our conversation and took the phone out of my pocket. There was a new red alert notification that reads –

"Rebecca has entered the last leg of her life. It's time to say goodbye" – in red and bold.

At first glance, I could not understand the notification. Then I realized and when I did, it shook the earth beneath my feet.

In the year 2075, Apple came up with a breakthrough technological advance that can predict the last few days of anyone's life based on historical data, AI, and astrological calculations. I have always been afraid of losing Rebecca, so I set up for her. It was so unexpected that my entire body froze for a few minutes.

"Is everything fine?" – Rebecca asked me while closing the zip of her luggage. I could hear that but was not in a condition to reply to anything.

I tapped the notification with a shaking finger. The wellness app opened and it showed the same message again with a smiling picture of her in the background. A drop of tears appeared in my eye but could not find its way.

At the bottom, there was a condition written in red – 'if you try to reveal it or alter it, your lifespan will become same as your loved one'.

'I have to be strong. I have to take care of our daughter' – this was the only thought I had in my mind. I could not look at my phone anymore. I switched it off forcefully and put it inside my pocket. I tried to be normal and talk as much as possible to my dearest wife, trying my best not to let her understand anything.

I saw her entering the gate and waving at me. I knew this is the last time I was seeing her. Many times, I thought in my mind - I wish this is just a bad dream. But I very well knew it was not. It was the reality, the harsh reality of life.

As soon as she disappeared from my sight, I felt so lonely and sick. In a hurry, I took out my phone, switched it on my phone, and called her immediately. The phone kept ringing. I kept calling her. I knew the phone was silent and she was going through the security check. I kept calling until she picks the call.

"Hello Eve, is everything fine? Did I leave anything?" – she was worried after she picked up the call for the thirteenth time.

"Me, you left me" – I said in a whisper.

"Aww!! My cutest hubby" – she teased.

"I Love You and I am going to Miss you so much" – I told closing my eyes.

"I Love You too. I will be back to you in a few months, don't worry at all" – she gave me a kiss.

I was silent and my eyes closed. I could not stand on my feet and sat on a table near the entry gate.

"I wish I could come with you" – I told her after a few moments.

"You stay with Emili and enjoy the cake" – she teased.

We kept talking until she boarded the flight. She was talking, I was mostly silent.

"I have to go now, the flight is about to take off, they are asking to switch off the phone" – she told me in a hurry.

'Mam, please switch off your phone'

No Please No – something inside me screamed.

"I will call you once I land and get some network there" – she told.

I opened the recorder on my phone to record her last "I Love You".

"Reb, I Love You" – I almost cried.

"Reb.."

'Rebb..'

-

The call got disconnected.

75 people died in that plane crash!!

IV

The Unsung Heroes

"Hey Mom, when are you coming, me and dad are waiting for you here. Come fast please, we have to cut the cake also" - the girl pleaded on her 9th birthday.

There was a lump in her throat, which she tries to gulp inside but could not. Tears started to roll down from her eyes. She resisted from showing the mother's weakness in front of the little one. Because, this is not the time to show weakness, it's time to be strong and fight the devil.

"Happy Birthday Darling" – she told and blew her a long kiss.

"Mamma is so sorry for not being there with you, but Mumma promises to be back soon." – she did not know whether she is telling her the truth or just giving the little girl some false hope. She also did not have any idea about what the future held. But she didn't want to make her little child disappointed.

The hardest thing to do is to choose between responsibility and family. Family is something for that you can die and responsibility is what you live for. And in the battle of life and death, only the braves stand out.

I was busy in the kitchen when I heard the bus stop in front of the gate honking two times. I was quite familiar with the honk by now. I opened the door and saw little kids coming out of the bus, all happy and laughing. I saw Milli coming down from the bus with Emilie and they started walking to cross the road towards the home. Seeing me standing at the front door, Milli started running towards me. Small footsteps one after another not willing to stop until it reaches her mama and hug her.

"School is closed till further notice" – she told joyfully hugging me and losing the bag from her back.

"Long Holiday.....Yayyyyy" – she continued.

I was listening to her while taking the school bag from her. I was happy seeing her excited about it but I knew the gravity of the news. Though it was expected considering the current situation that is going on all over the world. The kids must stay at home at any cost. I thought about the decision and it seemed to be the right thing to do. We both stood in our corridor and waved toward Emilie and her mom and came back home.

When Ethan came back from the office in the evening, Mili and I were sitting in the hall and I was teaching her how to draw a house beside a river. She sprung out off the sofa, ran, and jumped on him.

Ethan held her in his arms and pull her in his lap and she started telling him what she did the entire day - how she fed Tommy, our dog, how she helped me cooking pasta, how she drew her dream house, everything. Ethan listened to her calmly and appreciated all her work. He looked at me and smiled. He looked tired and stressed.

"Wash your hands properly and be ready for dinner" – I asked Milli. She blew a kiss to Ethan and went down from his lap and ran towards the washroom.

I took the bag from Ethan and asked, "Is everything fine?".

"Yeah almost. The business trip to France will get canceled. The flights are getting affected and they are deciding not to take risks. I have worked for the last two years on this presentation. Now, when it's so near, everything is on hold" – there was pain in his voice.

"Don't worry, everything will be fine" – I gave him a quick hug. He needed it.

"Get fresh and come. Dinner is ready; let's eat together" – I told.

Evan went to get fresh and I went to the kitchen to set up everything for dinner. We all were sitting in the dinner table and I was serving food to both of them. My phone started buzzing.

"I will get it" – Evan woke up and went to the hall to bring my phone.

"Who is that" – I asked Evan when he was coming to me holding my phone.

"From the hospital" – he replied while giving the phone to me.

I looked at the phone screen and kept the phone on my ear, "Hey Ramsey".

He started explaining to me the dire situation at the hospital and pleaded with me to come fast. I was silent. My hand was cold and I stopped feeling the weight of my phone. Evan and Milli were staring at me blankly, trying to understand what are wrong with me.

When the phone was cut and I came back to my senses. Evan asked, "Is everything fine?".

"I have to go to the hospital, right now" – I replied.

"But you took leave for two days" – Evan was still in shock.

"The situation is urgent there. They need me there" – I replied back.

"I will drop you" – Evan suggested.

"I will manage, please take care of Milli" – I went inside to get ready for the battle.

When I reached the hospital, it was uncharacteristically busy for a Thursday evening. It was 10 mins drive from Doctor's quarter to Hospital. I went straight to my cabin. When I reached the third floor and walked towards my cabin, I saw Ramsey waiting there for me. We both started walking towards the cabin.

"The four people who got admitted to the hospital in the morning are in bad condition mam" – he gave me an update while we were still walking in the corridor.

"Two of them had to be shifted to ICU and their condition is critical" – He told while I pushed open the door which was having my name written on it –

Rubi Mathew

Head of Medicine

The battle was long and I was inside ICU for almost 4 hours. But unfortunately, we could not bring both of them back to life. A young boy and a middle-aged man. We tried every possible way but the virus had made their body so weak that they stopped responding. I came out devasted and lost. Both the family of the patient was waiting outside. Maybe, this is the hardest part of being a doctor. Even after all your efforts, you are lost and then you have to break the devastating news all by yourself.

I went inside my cabin. Pulled the chair and sat on that, hiding my face behind my own hands. I looked at my own hands and tears rolled down from my eyes.

I felt the vibration of my phone on the table. I opened the drawer and saw 7 missed calls from Evan. I controlled my tears and made myself strong and decided not to be weak in front of him.

I took the phone and called him.

"Hello Evan" – I told; half of the words were still inside my throat only.

"What happened? Is everything alright?" – he asked with a worried voice.

I could not control myself, I burst out in tears.

"Hello, Rubi, tell me what happened. Are you alright?" – he was concerned about me.

"I tried Eve, I really tried but could not save them" - I busted into fresh tears.

"Who, what happened?" - he asked again.

I explained to him how we tried every possible way and their lifeless bodies stopped responding in front of my own eyes.

"I was there but could not help them" – I told with wet eyes, still trying to hold myself.

Evan listened to everything silently and replied in his comforting and compassionate voice, "Calm down Rub. I know you tried your best. You always do. Not everything is in your hands. Calm down please."

I was quiet. His calm voice made me calm down a bit and I stopped crying.

I heard a knock on my door.

"Come in."

"Mam, there are five more people with the same symptoms, and the two people who were already admitted last morning are having breathing problems. We may need to shift them to ICU." – Ramsey told in a flow and left.

I was still holding my phone to my ears and Evan heard Ramsey's voice.

"I have to go Eve" – I told with all the courage I had left my body.

"Take care" – He replied.

I kept the phone inside the drawer and rushed out of the door.

I called him the next morning around 6 o clock. He picked up the call in one ring. I can understand he was waiting for my call eagerly. By now many things have changed. Due to the drastic increase in covid cases and death toll, the government decided a complete lockdown. And the healthcare workers who were exposed to the virus on a regular basis were suggested to stay away from home and family. Which is quite obvious. The last thing you want in this critical condition was to become a potential carrier of the virus.

"Hello" – his sleepy but alert voice made me feel less anxious.

"Still awake?" – I asked in a low tone.

"Sort of" – he smiled to dilute the tension.

"Where is Milli?" – I asked.

"Right beside me, sleeping. Had a great difficulty to make her sleep yesterday night. Don't worry I will manage" – he told assuring.

"I know you will" - I replied.

"How is it going there?" – he asked hesitantly.

I wish he did not ask me this question when I was consciously trying to divert the topic.

"Not good, Eve. Things are pretty bad here and we are expecting it to be worse in the next few days" – I breathed a deep sigh.

"I called to inform you something"

"I won't be coming home for a few days"– I closed my eyes.

"I saw it on television last night. Please take care of yourself." – he told dishearteningly.

"I am going to make a delicious cake on Milli's birthday and You are going to miss it" – he teased me. I knew he was just trying to make me calm by diverting topics.

In this chaos and death, I completely forgot that tomorrow is Milli's birthday.

"I am so sorry Eve, I won't be able to meet her on her birthday. I am so sorry" – I was sobbing already.

"Rub, listen to me. Milli and Me both are so proud of you" – he told with so much love and compassion. I really touched my heart.

"I mean it." – he added.

The last two days in the hospital were hell. But it passed in a blink with the number of increased patients and the detrimental condition of the patients. I spend most of the time running from isolation wards to ICU and slept minimal hours in my cabin itself.

The overall condition has detreated drastically. The death count was also increasing sharply. And all the health care workers working tirelessly, continuously exposed to the threat of death, day and night.

I called Evan and asked him how he was doing. He told me that Milli was constantly looking for me from the morning. It shattered my heart and the motherhood in me was asking a legitimate questions about was this right to do or not. We both came up with a plan.

I took a break for an hour from the hospital and told Ramsey that I will be back within an hour. I called Evan before starting and asked him to be on the balcony with Milli.

It took me less than five minutes to reach outside of my quarter. It was one of the longest five minutes of my life full of anticipation and excitement to see my family. When you see death so closely, you love your loved ones even more.

I parked my Scotty and stood beneath the tree from where I can see Evan and Milli on my balcony. This was the same place where Evan used to stop and turn back and look at the balcony and blew a kiss every day while going to the office. The stream of memories just flowed in front of my eyes and bought tears.

I could see Evan opening the glass door with one hand and holding Milli with the other and coming to the balcony. We decided not to tell her about my guest appearance. Evan saw me and waved at me while Milli went inside to bring her favorite teddy bear. She was dressed in a white top, the one we bought last week for her birthday. How much it can change within a week.

I watched her play with her doll for some time while I was chatting with Evan.

"It's really very difficult to see her from far but not able to go and hold her in my arms"

"I can understand. Don't worry everything will be fine in some days."

"Eve, I miss you both a lot"

"We also miss you so much. Do you want to come inside? Is that fine?" – he asked.

Before I could think or reply anything, I hear Milli shouting excitedly,

"Mommyyy!!! Mommy!! see here" – she was waving both hands and the teddy bear fall down from her hand.

"Daddy, see, Mommy is here" – she pulled Evan's hand and showed him in my direction.

Evan was quiet.

I could not understand what I should do, first I tried to hide behind the tree, then I tried to hide my tears. I covered my face and sat on my Scotty and looked one last time towards the balcony. Milli was still waving at me. I busted out in tears. But I had to go. I made up my mind that I had to go now. I could still hear her voice asking for her mom to stop and meet her once on her birthday but her mom was helpless, so helpless that she can't even meet her on her birthday. I could see Milli in my side view mirror. Still waving her little hands toward me. Asking me to stop. But I can't. Maybe, I should have.

Little did I know; this was the last time I was seeing her.

V

The Incomplete Painting

The theory class for Fine Arts always bored him till the point of falling asleep. He always bunked those classes and take a direct auto from BHU gate to the Assi ghat. Then have a special tea at pappu tea shop and head towards the ghats. It was a cloudy afternoon with a soothing breeze and Aman Patel was absent that day.

His favorite thing to do when in ghat is to observe people and paint them. The afternoon breeze added more crowd in the ghat. All his favorite places were occupied. He kept walking while enjoying the cold breeze on his face. The scent of the scented candles, the smell of weed, occasional chanting of "Har Har Mahadev" - 'could not have been better'- he smiled and thought.

"Mein nehi ja raha kahin bhi, tum log jao PK sir ke class

karne" (You people go and attend PK sir's class, I am not going) - Paru rejected her friends' proposal to go back to class.

"Kya yar tum log yeh nazare chor ke class karne ja rahe ho" (how you guys can leave this place and go for class)

"Han sir hamare fan toh nehi hai tere tarah toh kya kare jana parega attendance keliye"

"Yeh toh hai" - Paru winked and told -

"Tum log chalo fir mein thoda enjoy karke a jayunga"(You guys carry on, I will come after sometime)

"Aur han PK sir ko mere taraf se namaste bol dena" - everyone laughed and left.

Paru sat there looking at the dark clouds on the horizon, feeling the moister of the river Ganga on her skin. Both her legs were dipped gently into the river. Her dark blue dress was matching the color of the water and was perfectly contrasting the dark clouds in the backdrop. Her long hair was floating around in the slow wind.

She dipped her legs in the cold water and looked up to the clouds in the sky. Her bright eyes were piercing through the darkness. She remembered nothing. Not that she didn't try but all the thoughts looked so meaningless in that setup. She simply sat there ignoring the people and their examining eyes. People started going back to their homes and stays expecting a thunderstorm.

"Is not it beautiful out here" – Paru got back to her senses with an unknown voice. When she opened her eyes, she saw a young boy sitting beside him with a smiling face admiring the beauty of nature just like she was doing with closed eyes. He was not looking at her though. He was looking straight at the horizon where folk of white birds was flying in hurry to go back to their nest.

"It is" – she nodded in affirmation. There was a welcome tone in her voice. They both stayed silent for a few seconds while a gust of cold wind made its way through them.

"What do you like the most about this place" - he asked with a genuine interest to know. This time he looked into her eyes.

'So beautiful' – he thought in his mind.

"The ghats and the cold water of Ganga" – she replied dangling her legs in the water. The anklet on her feet matched the sound of the water touching the ghats.

"You?" – she asked.

"I am Aman" – he replied.

She laughed. Her smile is so vibrant and warm.

"I asked what you like most about this place" – she giggled.

"Ohh, I thought" – he felt embarrassed.

"I love the energy of this place, how people think here, what they live by, whom they worship and everything about them" – he replied with glittering eyes.

"So, you are not from here" – she asked.

"No" – he replied.

"You come to ghat every day?" – he inquired.

"Not regularly, but sometimes. I choose windy days especially" – she tied her hair with her left hand and the tattoo of Trishul was visible to Aman.

"Har Har Mahadev" – he murmured.

A few raindrops started falling with thunder and lightning. She looked at the sky and took her feet out and started wearing her shoe.

"It was nice meeting you Amit, btw I am Paru" – she stood up.

"It was really nice meeting you Paru" – Aman beamed a smile.

She returned the smile back and with one moment of awkwardness she looked at Aman and started walking away from him. He was feeling like everything was coming to an end so abruptly. He wanted her to stay for some more time. He wanted to spend some more time with her. Yet she was leaving. He at least wanted to say bye to her properly.

"Paru" – he called her name. It was a rather urge for her to see her one last time.

Paru turned back and faced Aman. Aman walked towards her with her bag in his hand.

"Thank you so much, I completely forgot in hurry" – she told apologetically while taking the bag from him.

"It was nice meeting you" – he forwarded his hand and she shook his hand with gratitude.

She smiled and waved at him. Even the dark clouds laughed at him from above.

Paru reached her hostel just before it started raining very heavily. She liked the rain so much but did not want to get wet in the evening. She stood on her bed and searched for the locker key in her handbag. She looked at her bag and remembered Aman. She felt bad for not being able to thank him properly. She thought next time when she will meet him, she will take him to her favourite chai shop near the ghat. But she was not sure whether she will find Aman again or not.

Emerged in these thoughts, she pulled her bag and opened the chain.

There was an envelope inside. She took it out from the bag in surprise. There was a A4 size paper inside the envelope. When she looked at that, she was awestruck – it was a beautiful painting of a girl sitting on the ghat, putting her legs on the river. There were dark clouds in the back ground and girl was sitting on the step looking towards the sky. She started blushing realizing that the painting she is looking at is inspired by her.

After looking at the picture for some time, she realized the picture is not complete. She looked here and there on the page and then she turned the page –

"You are way more beautiful than any painting I will ever make." –

A. Patel

"Aman……."

Thank You